Don Bousquet's

NEXT BOOK

Covered Bridge Press
7 Adamsdale Road
N. Attleborough, MA 02760
(508) 761-7721

ISBN 0-924771-99-2

10 9 8 7 6 5 4 3 2 1

Don Bousquet
At Home in Rhode Island

IF SUPERMAN WERE FROM RHODE ISLAND

RECENTLY SIGHTED IN NARRAGANSETT BAY:
THE LOCH NESS MOBSTER

DOUG WHITE, 7 AM

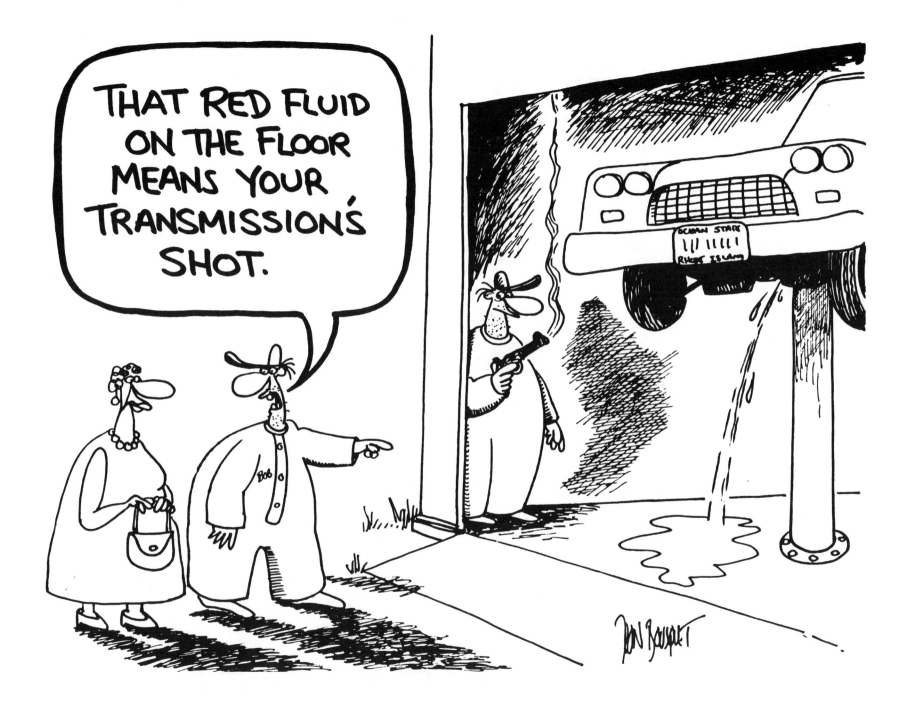

THE BLOCK ISLAND BOAT'S PRESIDENTIAL SUITE

A RHODE ISLANDER ABOARD THE TITANIC

HELLO. YOU HAVE REACHED THE ORGANIZED CRIME CAPITOL OF NEW ENGLAND... IF YOU NEED TO HAVE AN ASSOCIATE "SLEEP WITH THE FISHES" PRESS ONE, NOW... IF YOU WOULD LIKE TO HAVE HIM FOUND IN THE TRUNK OF A '78 COUPE DEVILLE PRESS TWO, NOW... IF YOU WOULD....
DON BOUSQUET

Don Bousquet
Down by the Sea

HE INSTRUCTED ME TO BUILD A VESSEL SO MANY CUBITS BY SO MANY CUBITS BUT IT WAS MY IDEA TO WRAP HER IN FIBERGLASS!
DON BOUSQUET

Don Bousquet
At the Casino

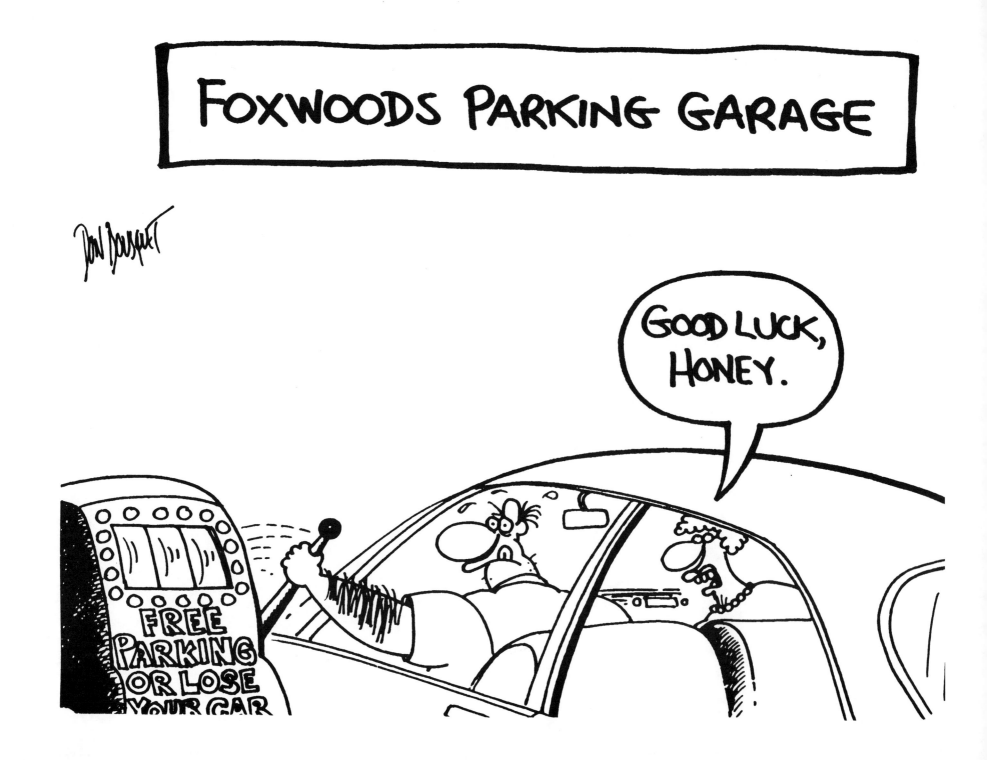

Don Bousquet
At Large in the World

BAD CASE OF TEACHER BURNOUT

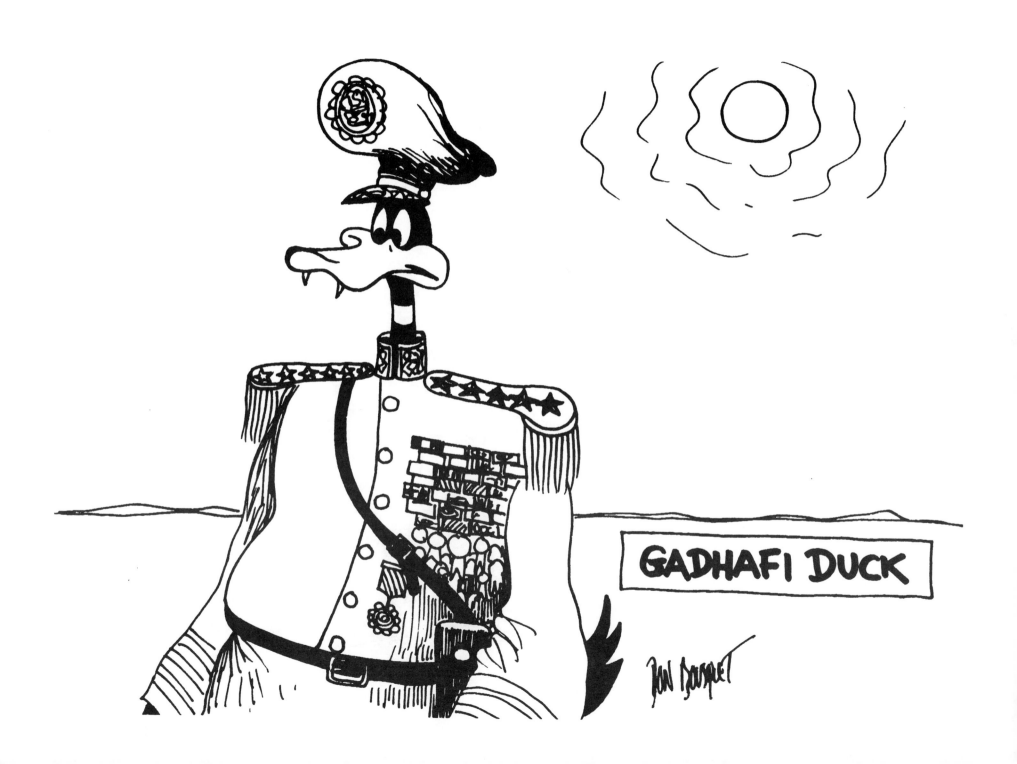

GADHAFI DUCK

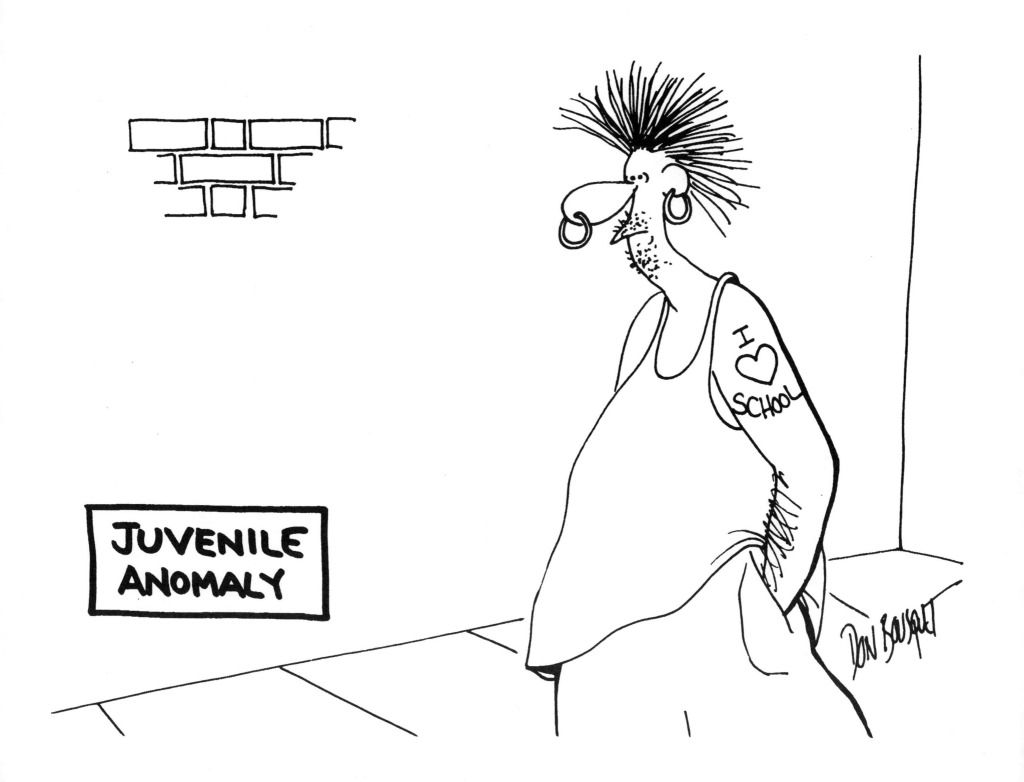

Don Bousquet
In Outer Space

THE VISITORS HAD SIGNALED THEIR PEACEFUL INTENTIONS AND IT SEEMED THAT A NEW ERA OF WORLDWIDE PROSPERITY WAS AT HAND. THEN AS THE ALIEN CRAFT SETTLED TO THE SURFACE OF ROUTE 1 IN EAST GREENWICH, A LANDING GEAR LEG CAUGHT THE EDGE OF A POTHOLE...